ADVENTURES
AT
HOUND HOTEL

raintree

Raintree is an imprint of Capstone Global Library Limited, a company incorporated in England and Wales having its registered office at 7 Pilgrim Street, London, EC4V 6LB – Registered company number: 6695582

**www.raintree.co.uk**
myorders@raintree.co.uk

Edited by Clare Lewis and Julie Gassman
Designed by Russell Griesmer
Original illustrations © Capstone Global Library Limited 2015
Illustrated by Deborah Melmon
Production by Charmaine Whitman
Originated by Capstone Global Library
Printed and bound in China.

ISBN 978-1-4062-9228-2 (paperback)
18  17  16  15  14
10 9 8 7 6 5 4 3 2 1

**British Library Cataloguing in Publication Data**
A full catalogue record for this book is available from the British Library.

# Homesick Herbie

by Shelley Swanson Sateren

illustrated by Deborah Melmon

# CONTENTS

# ADVENTURES AT HOUND HOTEL

## IT'S TIME FOR YOUR ADVENTURE AT HOUND HOTEL!

At Hound Hotel, dogs are given the royal treatment. We are a top-notch boarding kennel. When your dog stays with us, we will follow your feeding schedule, take them for walks and tuck them into bed at night.

We are just a short walk away from the dogs — the kennels are located in a heated building at the end of our driveway. Every dog has his or her own kennel, with a bed, blanket and water bowl.

Rest assured ... a stay at the Hound Hotel is like a holiday for your dog. We have a large playground, plenty of toys and a pool for the dogs to play in, in the summer. Your dog will love playing with the other guests.

# HOUND HOTEL
# WHO'S WHO

### WINIFRED WOLFE

Hound Hotel is run by Winifred Wolfe, a lifelong dog lover. Winifred loves all types of dogs. She likes to get to know every breed. When she's not taking care of the canines, she writes books about — that's right — dogs.

### ALFIE AND ALFREEDA WOLFE

Winifred's twins help out as much as they can. Whether your dog needs gentle attention or extra playtime, Alfreeda and Alfie provide special services you can't find anywhere else. Your dog will never get bored whilst these two are helping out.

### WOLFGANG WOLFE

Winifred's husband helps out at the hotel whenever he can, but he spends most of his time travelling to study packs of wolves. Wolfgang is a real wolf lover — he even named his children after pack leaders, the alpha wolves. Every wolf pack has two alpha wolves: a male wolf and a female wolf, just like the Wolfe family twins.

Next time your family goes on holiday, bring your dog to Hound Hotel.

Your pooch is sure to have a howling good time!

# CHAPTER 1
## Silly clothes on little dogs

I'm Alfie Wolfe, and there's one thing I hate.
Bows on dogs.

Another thing I hate – tiny little clothes
on tiny little dogs. Have you ever seen a dog
in clothes? Some dog owners are crazy! Boy
or girl dog, it doesn't matter. I just don't
understand why people dress dogs up.

You won't believe what Herbie was wearing
the first time I met him. I have never felt more
sorry for a dog.

Herbie checked into Hound Hotel last year. Last summer to be exact. Last July to be even more exact.

My dad had just left for a whole month. His longest wolf-study trip yet. Gosh, I missed him. But that's not the point.

Back to Herbie.

Of course, he's not the only dog that's come to our hotel wearing silly clothes. But he goes down in history as the *worst* dressed dog. Trust me.

I always try to take off dogs' bows and stuff, as soon as their owners leave. But my sister has fast fingers. (She has fast everything, if you want to know the truth – hands, legs, mouth.) I'd turn my back for a second, and she'd put those silly bows straight back onto the dogs.

Here's the thing: every type of dog in the

world originally came from wolves. Every dog's great-great-great (add a lot more greats here) grandparents were wolves. Would you put a pink dress and bow on a wolf?

If your answer is no, good for you! If your answer is yes, I feel *so* sorry for your dog.

But back to Herbie. I'll tell you all about him, whether you put bows in your dog's hair or not.

Herbie arrived on a Friday morning. The day had begun quite normally. Spot, our cockerel, woke me up the second the sun rose. I woke up in a pile of pillows on the living room floor. Being asleep on the floor is normal, in the summertime anyway. It's normal for my mum and sister, too.

We'd fallen asleep watching another dog film. Mum was on the sofa, stretching. Alfreeda was next to me on the floor, drooling all over a pillow. My sister drools as much as a bloodhound. *Ugh.* Disgusting!

I poked her awake, and we got up straight away. You can't be lazy when you run a dog hotel.

We had breakfast on the kitchen floor. That's normal in our house, too.

Mum was writing another book about dogs. As usual, the kitchen table and chairs were covered with her writing things.

We wolfed down our cereal. I chucked my bowl into the sink.

Alfreeda put hers in the dishwasher. Then she wiped milk off the worktop really quickly. And swept crumbs off of the floor. And emptied the dustpan into the rubbish bin. And hung the broom up in the utility room.

She did all of this in about two minutes flat. She wasn't even out of breath. She's just really quick.

"Good girl, Alfreeda!" Mum said. She patted my sister on the head.

Not once.

Not twice.

Three times, as if Alfreeda had just fetched a stick from the edge of a valley in two minutes flat. *Ugh*. My sister! Always trying to be top dog. I hated it!

I popped my bowl into the dishwasher. It landed a bit wonky.

"Good boy, Alfie," Mum said.

I got one pat on the head.

Mum handed us our dog brushes for our poodle-like hair. Our hair is really thick and curly and crazy. You can't get a comb through it, and it's really hard to brush.

So my sister and I use dog brushes – the kind that you use for big grooming jobs on big furry dogs. Those big brushes are the only things that can handle our hair.

Alfreeda and I always race to finish first. I won't say who always wins. But you can probably guess.

Well, I can't help it. My brush always gets completely stuck, and Mum has to come to my rescue.

Somehow, Alfreeda's brush speeds through her hair. She even has time to put in bows and clips and stuff.

Like I said before, I hate bows on dogs. But I am sort of glad that my sister wears them. Otherwise we'd look almost completely alike. *Ugh!*

At last, Mum said, "That's enough." She put down my brush.

She clapped her hands together, like she does at the beginning of every business day.

"All right, gang!" she said. "We've got some wonderful four-legged visitors waking up to another day. What kind of day are we going to give them?"

"Fun," I said.

"The best day ever!" Alfreeda shouted.

Mum smiled at her with a huge grin. She patted Alfreeda on the head again.

Suddenly Mum's mobile phone rang. She grabbed it from the charger.

"Hello!" she said, as cheerful as ever. "This is Hound Hotel. Winifred Wolfe speaking. How may I help you?"

Mum explained to someone how to find our hotel. Then she said, "We can't wait to meet Herbie! See you soon! Goodbye."

"Who was that?" I asked.

"Ms Frill," Mum said. "Her little Herbie is coming to stay with us for the weekend. She called to say they are on their way. Herbie's a little Yorkshire terrier."

"A Yorkie!" Alfreeda cried.

Trust my sister to know that kind of terrier's nickname.

"We've never had a Yorkie here!" Alfreeda shouted and jumped around. "They're the sweetest little dogs on the planet!"

She stopped jumping. She turned to me.

"Herbie's mine," she said in her top-dog voice. "I want to play with him first."

"No!" I said. "I do!"

A dog that little would be so much fun. He could ride on my toy rocket. And we could play camping. I could make him a sleeping bag out of one of Dad's socks!

"Don't be silly, you two," Mum said. She walked towards the back door. "You can share playtime with Herbie. He's coming to stay with us for three days."

Alfreeda narrowed her eyes at me. "No," she whispered in my ear. "There won't be enough of that little dog to share. Come on. Race you!"

We sprinted down our long driveway, all the way to the kennel building.

I won't say who reached the front door first.

## — CHAPTER 2 —
# Herbie Boo Boo

The race didn't end at the front door. Alfreeda charged through the kennel building. I chased after her.

Through the office. Down the hallway. Past the storeroom. Through the utility room. Past the kitchen. Through the grooming room.

Alfreeda dashed into the big room at the back of the building. That's where all of the dog pens are. (Or you can call them kennels. Take your pick.)

I won't say who got there first. But that someone shouted, "I've won!" and woke up every single dog.

They all jumped off of their beds and started to bark.

"Hey, you lot," I shouted.

"Good morning, you wonderful, beautiful creatures!" Alfreeda called to them.

She beat me to the MP3 player.

"Play some jazz music," I said. "The blues. That would be so cool."

"No," she said. "It's a sunny day. Our guests need happy music to wake up to!"

She says that every morning, even if it's raining. It's annoying.

I like the blues. My dad does, too. I really miss my dad.

My sister was already on top of a chair. She reached up to the shelf and pressed buttons on the MP3 player. She *always* played the same silly pop song.

I just stood there and watched. It's not as though I could've shoved her off of the chair. That would get me into far too much trouble. And I wanted to play with that Yorkie!

The song started. I groaned. The words went like this: "Oh baby. It's a sunshiny day. A baby-blue-sky day. Together baby, you and I, we're happy. So happy, happy, happy…"

The singer sings "happy" about twenty times. Then he sings all of the words all over again. Then he sings "happy" about twenty times more after that. I'm not joking. A dog could have easily written that song.

"Thank you, Alfreeda!" Mum called. She was busy giving the dogs their breakfast. "I love that song. It starts the day on such a cheerful note. Play it again!"

*Ughh!* I just wanted to plug my fingers in my ears. But I needed my fingers for all the jobs I had to do. Alfreeda and I had to fill the dogs' water bowls. The race was on.

Alfreeda leapt from kennel to sink. From sink to kennel. She filled six water bowls in about six minutes flat. I almost filled one. I can't help it. I'm a little bit clumsy, and I trip and spill the water sometimes. Give me a break!

Mum always makes me wipe up the floor. I was still wiping when Alfreeda shouted, "Finished!"

I couldn't believe my eyeballs. She had already finished preparing Herbie's kennel! A little bed sat in the corner. There was a little Hound Hotel blanket folded neatly on top. The little water bowl was sparkling clean. Of course it was filled right to the top with nice fresh water. There was even a little pillow with a tiny bone-shaped treat on top. It was just waiting, and looking really tasty, for our newest hotel guest.

She'd even made a sign. It read:

The letters weren't even messy.

"It's not fair," I said. "I don't have time to make a sign."

That second, the office doorbell rang. It sounds like a barking dog: *Yap! Yap! Yap!* You can hear it all over the kennel building. All of the dogs started to bark again. They always do when the doorbell rings.

Of course Alfreeda beat me to the office. I had to finish wiping up the silly floor.

When I got there, a lady was already sitting on the bench. That's where guests sit. The human ones. Their dogs usually sit on the floor.

Mum sat at the desk, behind her computer.

A tiny dog suitcase sat on the desk next to her. I'd never seen one so small.

Sitting at the other end of the bench was a tall, glamorous lady. Ms Frill, I assumed.

Ms Frill wore a sparkly hat with a feather poked through the top. She had a sparkly dress on and shoes that matched too. The fancy shoes had really high heels. She was a very tall lady to have such a short dog.

Ms Frill's handbag sat beside her on the
bench, between Ms Frill and Alfreeda. The
purse was big and pink and sparkly. A tiny dog's
head poked out of the top. It looked like a toy.
I mean, *he* looked like a toy. But he was real,
that's for sure. And he had a big blue bow on
top of his tiny head.

He wore a tiny little collar that said "SWEET BABY" on it. Alfreeda went all ooey-gooey.

"Oh, Herbie," she cooed in her talking-to-babies voice. "You're *soooo* lovely! I knew you would be!"

She rubbed her nose against his. Disgusting! Not Herbie's nose. My sister's!

"Can I pick him up?" Alfreeda begged. "Please?"

Ms Frill took Herbie out of the handbag and put him on her own lap. She held him tightly and patted his head.

That's when I was nearly sick.

Herbie wore a blue, baby-sized t-shirt. It had sparkly silver letters on the front that said "MUMMY'S BABY."

I was too disgusted to talk.

"I'm *sooo* worried that my darling angel is going to miss me *sooo* much," Ms Frill said in a talking-to-babies voice. "Aren't you, Herbie Boo Boo? I just know you'll be *sooo* homesick. Oh, my darling baby, boo hoo…"

Mum was standing next to Ms Frill now. Mum gently patted her shoulder. Ms Frill sniffed. Mum handed her a tissue. Ms Frill blew her nose. She handed the tissue back to Mum. Mum smiled her anything-for-a-guest smile.

"Don't worry, Ms Frill," Alfreeda said. "I'll keep Herbie company while you're away. I'll play with him every minute of the day. I'll make sure he isn't lonely!"

"Thank you, dear," Ms Frill said. She shook her head sadly. "But I've never left my baby for this long. This is *sooo* hard for both of us, isn't it, Herbie Boo Boo?"

She kissed him about twenty times all over his face. She kissed his paws, too.

Suddenly I didn't want to play with Herbie anymore.

No.

I wanted to *rescue* him. From his life.

## CHAPTER 3
# Unpacking the tiny suitcase

Ms Frill really didn't want to leave. She'd cry *goodbyyyyyye* to Herbie. She'd go out to her car. Then she'd come running back into the office to say goodbye again!

She did that five times!

Every time, she'd say something really soppy like, "When you get lonely, Herbie darling, just look at my picture."

Mum went to the storeroom for another box of tissues. The rubbish bin was overflowing with used ones. Mum finally took hold of

Ms Frill's arm and personally walked her to her car. Then Mum personally helped Ms Frill into her car. She gave her one last tissue. Then Mum stood in front of Ms Frill's car door, so she couldn't get out.

Alfreeda stood at the window with Herbie, watching it all. She held Herbie and his tiny suitcase. For some reason, Ms Frill had handed both of these things to my sister instead of me!

The only thing Ms Frill had given to me was a little piece of paper. It was a new-visitor form. Ms Frill's elegant writing covered it. There was lots of information about Herbie written all over it.

I didn't understand Ms Frill. Why hadn't she put Herbie into *my* arms? I was a boy. Herbie was a boy. That little dog needed some proper boy time, and I was his man.

"Let me hold him," I said.

"No," Alfreeda said and laughed. "He wants me, can't you see?"

She made his front leg wave. "That's it, Herbie, sweetie," she said in that awful talking-to-babies voice. "Wave bye-bye. Your mummy's driving away. Look! Zoom! There she goes!"

Straight away, Herbie started to cry quiet little cries. Lots of them, one on top of the other. His stomach went in and out with every cry, like waves in a swimming pool.

"Why did you do that?" I demanded. "You made him watch his mum leave? You made him cry!"

"Alfie," she said in her teacher voice. "What do *you* do every time Dad leaves for Canada? You won't let Mum leave the airport! Not till Dad's plane is a speck in the sky!"

That told me.

But Herbie kept crying. Soft little sobs. Loads of them. They were so squeaky. Like a baby mouse that's lost its mother.

The truth is, that's just how I feel when Dad leaves. On the first day, at least. But that's not the point.

"*Shh*, Herbie Boo Boo," Alfreeda said and rocked him. "You'll be absolutely fine. You and I, we'll have lots of fun. You'll see!"

She marched to Herbie's kennel. I followed. She put Herbie on top of his little bed and covered him with the little Hound Hotel blanket. She made sure his head was on the little pillow. His nose touched the treat, but he didn't even sniff it. He didn't even move. He just kept sobbing.

I couldn't stand seeing him like that, so I ran to the storeroom and found a little red ball. I ran back with it and dropped it on the floor, right in front of his bed. Herbie didn't even lift his chin. I caught the ball as it bounced and dropped it again.

Alfreeda rolled her eyes. "Stop that," she said.

"No!" I bounced the ball again. "Come on, little one. Let's play!"

Herbie stared at the little bone treat. I couldn't believe he wouldn't eat it.

I bounced the ball again.

Alfreeda rolled her eyes again. I wished

those eyes would roll out of her head and down a drain sometimes.

"So, Alfie," she said in her teacher voice. "What do *you* normally feel like doing, after Dad goes on his trips?"

"Well, um, lie around, I suppose," I said. "And sleep."

*And cry sometimes,* I thought.

"Exactly," she said.

She picked up Herbie. She wrapped the blanket around him. She rocked him and started to sing, "Twinkle, twinkle, little star."

Herbie kept crying.

"He needs to go outside," I said.

"Not yet," Alfreeda said. "He needs to be able to feel sad first. That's right, little one. Have a good cry."

She rocked him and sang, "Mary had a little lamb…" That poor dog. I was feeling sorrier for him by the second!

"Okay," I said. "I'll unpack his suitcase. Then we're going outside."

I grabbed the little suitcase. It was baby blue and had little sparkly puppies all over it.

I unzipped it and pulled out a baby-blue doggie sweater. It had sparkly purple letters on the front that said, "My heart belongs to my mummy!"

*Ughh!* I dropped it onto the floor.

"Ooh, you'll look so sweet in that, Herbie Boo Boo," Alfreeda cooed.

Herbie didn't answer. Not just because he's a dog and can't talk, but because he'd fallen asleep in Alfreeda's arms.

She kept rocking him. She started to sing, really softly, "Row, row, row your boat…"

I unpacked the rest of Herbie's stuff. I couldn't believe my eyeballs.

Ms Frill had packed baby food for him. That's right. Food for human babies. In tiny little jars … fruit … and vegetables.

"Yikes," I said. "That's really strange."

Alfreeda's eyebrows went up. She didn't say anything.

"Come on," I said. "Don't tell me that you don't think that's a bit strange."

She still didn't say anything.

Ha! I had her there.

Next, I pulled out a doggie chew toy. It was in the shape of a baby's bottle. I. Am. Not. Joking.

"Strange!" I said and I threw it across the kennel.

Then I pulled out something peculiar.

"Ew!" I said. "What is this?"

Actually, I knew what it was: a lady's nightgown!

"Disgusting!"
I threw it over
my shoulder and
shivered.

"*Shh*," Alfreeda said.
"You'll wake him up.
And for your information,
Ms Frill sent that because
it *smells* like her. It will make
Herbie will feel more at home."

"I don't care," I said. "A lady's nightgown is still pretty disgusting!"

I dug to the bottom of the suitcase.

"No more toys?" I said.

The last thing I found was a picture of Ms Frill in a silver frame.

Alfreeda looked at it. Suddenly she put Herbie in my arms. "Hold him," she ordered. "Don't wake him up. I'll be back soon." She ran out of the kennel room.

I stared at the furry-faced little man in my arms. He was actually really sweet.

I started to wish that I had a Yorkie. One of my own. One I could keep in my room, away from Alfreeda.

But my dad isn't that keen on little dogs. He likes big dogs like wolves.

That's why Mum had opened Hound Hotel. She loves all sorts of dogs – big, little, and everything in between. She adores them all, and one or two family dogs would never be enough.

"Where did that silly Alfreeda go, *hmm?*" I asked in a voice as soft as his silky hair.

I started to rock him, backwards and forwards, like a tree branch on a windy day.

I started to sing, "Hush, litle baby…"

My voice came out wrong. A bit like a howling beagle. Herbie woke up straight away. His eyes opened wide. He lifted his little head. He looked around. I could tell he didn't know where on earth he was.

Then, he started to howl *really* loudly!

## ⟝ CHAPTER 4 ⟞
# Come on, Herbie

A minute later, Alfreeda raced into Herbie's kennel. The little dog was crying his heart out.

"What have you done to him?" she demanded.

"Nothing!" I said.

She was carrying a little purple table. It came from her bedroom. Normally, she kept some of her stuffed dogs on it. She had hundreds.

She put the table in the corner and sat Ms Frill's photograph on top of it. Then she took Herbie off me.

"It's okay, baby," she cooed in his ear.

"He is *not* a baby," I said.

"Well, Alfie," Alfreeda said in her school teacher voice, "his mum treats him like one. So *we* have to. Then he'll feel more at home. Make sense?"

She had a point.

"Look, Herbie!" Alfreeda pointed at Ms Frill's picture. "There's your mummy! Just look at her whenever you feel sad. She's here with you!"

Herbie stared at the picture. He fell completely silent.

"Told you," Alfreeda said to me. "No more crying."

Herbie kept staring at his mum. I looked at him.

Then my mouth must've fallen open because Alfreeda said, "What?"

I pointed at Herbie. "Wow," I said. "I've *never* seen a dog do that."

My sister and I looked closer.

The poor little thing was really crying.

I mean, he had real tears! Wet ones! The hair under his eyes was getting *wet*!

"That's it," I said. I grabbed him from Alfreeda. "Come on, Herbie. We're going outside."

☙ ☙ ☙

I thought that some fresh air would do him good. And maybe a game of catch. Anything to take his mind off his mum.

That's the kind of thing my mum says to me whenever Dad leaves. And what do I usually do? Roll over in my bed and pull a pillow over my head. But that's not the point. It was time for Herbie to have some fun.

I carried him out into the playground. That's a big fenced-in place where the dogs can play. It's covered in grass and full of dog toys. It even has a dog slide and a dog pool. They're actually made for toddlers – human ones – but only dogs are allowed in ours.

I put Herbie on the grass and grabbed a Frisbee. I threw it. Not hard. Not far.

"Come on, Herb!" I said. "Go and get it!" It should have been really easy for him to catch. But did he even try?

He didn't even sit up. He didn't even look at the Frisbee.

He stared at a rock.

"Come on, Herb." I propped up his back legs.

He slumped back down. He sat on his bottom and wouldn't move.

"Would you like to have a go on the slide?" I asked. "I'll help you up. You'll zoom down! It's so much fun! Come on!"

He started to whimper all over again!

He was like a crying machine with a very powerful engine.

I used to cry like that when I was little. And maybe even now when I get really upset.

(Like whenever Dad goes to Canada to study the wolves.)

Alfreeda kneeled beside us. She stared at Herbie. I stared at him, too.

Then I stared at my sister. She's never normally quiet.

Then she went really strange. Her eyes went all sparkly. She looked like she'd just seen a really bright light bulb switch on, just above her head. That meant she had an idea.

I thought, *Uh-oh. Here we go again.*

## CHAPTER 5

# Hold your horses

Alfreeda didn't waste a second. She picked Herbie up and carried him inside the kennel building. I followed.

"What are doing?" I demanded. "He was just about to fetch the Frisbee."

"Really?" she asked. "Just like you get over it so quickly after Dad's left. I always suggest fun things to do and you always say, 'Go away.'" She laughed.

"It's not funny," I said.

"I know it isn't," she said. "I take that laugh back. Stay with him. I'll be back soon."

She ran off.

Herbie stared at his mum's picture. He just kept sobbing.

This was not much fun.

I stared at the dogs in the other kennels. I could've been playing with a beagle. Or a bulldog.

Or a huge furry wolfhound! I looked at that big dog and started to think. *That big dog and I, we could play prehistoric games. I could be the caveman. He could be the woolly mammoth ... No! I can't abandon Herbie. He needs me!*

I started to pat Herbie, really gently. He kept crying, as though his little heart would break in two.

"*Shh*," I said. "It's okay. You'll see your mum in three days. Then you can tell her all about the fun time you've had here!"

Herbie stopped crying. He looked at me. He tilted his head.

It's as though he was asking me, "Fun? What fun?"

I nodded and said, "You're right. Let's get this party started. First, let's get rid of this stuff."

Fast as a greyhound at a racetrack, I put his mum's photograph into his suitcase. Then the baby food jars and the bib.

"We serve real food at this here country café," I said in my best cowboy voice.

Then I took off his hair bow, his baby shirt and his collar. I popped them into his suitcase. I threw in the awful baby-bottle chew toy, too. I didn't touch the nightgown. *Yuck.* Then I zipped it up and carried the suitcase to the storeroom. I left it there.

I went back to Herbie and said, "That's better! Look, you're a normal dog now. See?"

I threw the water out of his water bowl. I turned it upside down. Instant mirror. "Look," I said.

Herbie stared at himself. Then I couldn't believe my eardrums.

He yapped! He actually *yapped*!

*A happy-dog yap!*

He put his nose right up to the shiny metal. He pawed at the dog bowl. The dish flew across the kennel. It hit the fence then dropped onto the floor. Herbie immediately started crying again.

As quickly as a runaway horse, I began talking in my cowboy voice again. "Whoa there, little man. Hold your horses! I'll go and find my little old toy horsey on wheels. I'll take you on a wild ride around this here ranch, okey dokey? I'll be right back."

I sprinted outside and into our garage. I dug and dug and chucked and threw. I couldn't find my old toy horsey on wheels anywhere! I finally gave up and headed back to Herbie's kennel.

I took a look around then shouted at my sister, "What have you *done* to this place?"

Alfreeda grinned at me. "Do you like it?" she asked. "It's Herbie's baby nursery."

All of the rubbish was back out of Herbie's suitcase. But that's not all. The kennel was packed with stuffed dogs. She'd brought down my old blue high chair too. You know, the kind babies sit in to eat. Herbie was sitting in it. I stared at him.

I couldn't believe my eyeballs. "Where did you get that?" I demanded.

Herbie was wearing a little sailor suit. It had a matching shirt, trousers and hat. I had to admit that Herbie looked quite sweet in it. But that's not the point. That was *my* sailor suit! I'd seen it in my baby pictures!

"Tell me! Where did you find it?" I demanded.

"In the attic!" Alfreeda said and grinned. "I

couldn't believe it. I found all our baby stuff up there! I didn't know Mum and Dad had kept it!"

Suddenly, I'd had enough. "Hey," I said.

"What?" she said.

"Do you know how old Herbie is?" I asked.

She shook her head.

"He's six!" I shouted. "I read his information form! Six people years! How many *dog* years is that?"

"Um," she said, "let's think. Six times seven. Okay, um. Forty-two?"

Wow. How did she work that out so quickly?

I had no idea if forty-two was the right answer. But I acted as though it was.

"That's right!" I said. "He's *not* a baby! Stop

treating him like one, or he'll hate it here! His mummy will be able to tell. She'll never bring him back!"

That stopped my sister in her tracks.

"Hold tight, Herb, old boy," I said. "Alfie will be back soon to save the day."

Then I ran to the house and up to the attic.

I was going to find my horsey on wheels!

## ☐— CHAPTER 6 —☐
# The Alfie male

"Gosh, Alfreeda has made a mess up here," I said.

I was talking to my horsey on wheels. I held him in my arms.

My sister had emptied out loads of boxes, and all sorts of things covered the attic floor.

"Mum's going to make her clean this up," I said. "I don't suppose Alfreeda will care anyway. She does everything so quickly. It drives me mad!"

Horsey didn't say anything. Take it from me. Friendship with a stuffed toy only goes so far. I kicked the mess out of the way, trying to get back to the door.

Suddenly I spied something. Two things, I mean. Two tiny baby t-shirts. One pink, one blue.

The pink one said, "ALFREEDA FEMALE."

The blue one said, "ALFIE MALE."

"Was I really that little once?" I asked my toy horsey. "I must've looked so sweet in that tiny t-shirt."

I read the words out loud, "Alfie Male."

Suddenly it hit me. Something I'd never thought about before.

ALFIE MALE. Get it? As in, "Alpha Male."

ALFREEDA FEMALE. Get it? Yes! "Alpha Female."

Trust my parents to do something that bizarre.

You see, every wolf pack in the world has them. A boy leader and a girl leader. "Alpha" means "first" or "top." As in, "top dog."

The Alpha Male and Alpha Female are the biggest, cleverest, bravest, strongest wolves in their pack. And yes, the fastest. They look after the whole pack.

"Do you know what, Horsey?" I said. "I think my parents wanted my sister and me to be born leaders. Both of us. Not just the one born five minutes before me."

I gave Horsey a good stroke up and down his nose.

"Buck up, old boy," I said in my cowboy voice. "It's time to show a little dog a wild good time on this here ranch. Giddyup!"

I grabbed my old baby cowboy hat off of the floor. Then I sprinted to the kennels, as fast as a wild pony, racing over the moors.

## CHAPTER 7
# Jump on, little cowdog!

Two minutes later, Alfreeda took one look at Horsey and rolled her eyes.

"No way," she said. "Herbie's *not* going for a ride on that. He'll fall off straight away!"

She had a good point.

She also had one of the world's fastest brains.

She snapped her fingers. "I'll make a saddle!" she said.

In about four minutes flat, she had constructed a cardboard saddle. It was tied up around the horse nice and tightly with lots of tape.

She patted the finished saddle. "Jump on, little cowdog!" she said in her cowgirl voice.

Then I couldn't believe my eyeballs. Herbie jumped right onto the saddle!

"Yee-haw!" I said. "Giddyup!" And Herbie started to ride the horse from room to room. I pushed. Alfreeda galloped along on her hands and knees, right next to us.

And listen to this: The little cowdog didn't just sit on that saddle. He stood on his back legs and put his front paws on top of Horsey's head!

"Now you can see the whole ranch, little fellow," I said, panting as I pushed. "Jump off now and check your cows. Make sure no wolves got 'em in the night. Giddyup!"

We galloped right past Mum. She was talking to some guests in the office. We galloped through all the rooms again. Herbie barked and barked. He was the happiest cowdog in the whole Wild West!

"If only your mummy could see you now!" Alfreeda cried.

We galloped through the office again, down the hallway, and right past Mum.

Mum was leading a little Maltese called Muffin towards her pen. Muffin had stayed with us before.

"Hi, Muffin!" I called as I galloped past.

"Welcome back, Muffin!" Alfreeda said, galloping fast.

Suddenly, Herbie leapt off the saddle.

"Whoa, Horsey!" I cried. "We've lost our rider!"

Alfreeda and I stopped. We looked back. There stood Herbie, nose to nose with Muffin. Old Herb was wagging his tail like mad.

# ❧ CHAPTER 8 ❧
# Baby-blue-sky day

Five minutes later, Horsey sat in a corner of the storeroom. Alfreeda and I were out in the playground. So were the two new little best friends.

They kept rolling around and running in circles. And chasing each other's tails. And jumping on top of each other. Herbie kept yapping that happy-dog yap.

I sighed. Then I tried again to throw the ball. "Come on, Herb, old boy," I called. "Catch it!"

It was like he'd forgotten I was even existed. I really hoped my dad wouldn't forget about me — he was away for a whole month after all.

I went over to the big old tree. Alfreeda was lying under it in the shade. I sat next to her.

"This is so boring," she said. "If only we had another horse Muffin could ride."

"Yeah." A fly landed on my nose. I blew it away. A cow mooed somewhere.

"I suppose Herbie really likes playing with another small dog," I said.

Alfreeda sat up quickly. "What's the matter with him?" she demanded. "Aren't we good enough?"

"We're children, not dogs," I said.

"Sometimes I forget that," she said.

Suddenly I snapped my fingers. "Hey!" I said.

"Maybe that's what Herbie saw in the mirror! I mean, the bottom of his water bowl! He thought he'd seen another little dog to play with!"

Alfreeda wrinkled up her face. "What are you talking about?" she said. "You're so strange, Alfie Wolfe."

"You're stranger, Alfreeda Wolfe," I said.

The annoying stupid fly landed on my nose again. I swatted it away. A chicken clucked somewhere.

I started to think. *I suppose that's what I need the most too when Dad is away. A friend to play with.*

It's a shame I didn't have any friends around. All of mine lived in town.

"It's hot," Alfreeda said.

"We should fill up the dog pool," I said. "My old baby boat is in the attic."

"We could turn the boat into a pirate ship," she said.

"Why don't we dress Herbie up like a pirate?" I asked. "He'd just about fit into that little boat."

"We could dress Muffin up too," she said. "Like a girl pirate. We could use our old baby bath as a pirate ship. Both dogs should fit into that."

"Yes," I said.

Alfreeda jumped up.

"Keep an eye on them," she said in her top-dog voice. "Fill up the pool. I'll go and get the pirate stuff."

"Aye, aye, matey," I said in my best pirate voice. It was growly and rough and from deep inside my tummy.

"Oh, and grab my pirate costume, too," I said. "I'll be Captain Hook."

"No!" she said. "I want to!" My sister and I both dressed up as Captain Hook last Halloween.

Just then, something really strange happened. I couldn't believe my eyeballs.

Nice and slowly, Alfreeda shrugged. Then I couldn't believe my eardrums. "Okay," she said. "You can be Captain."

I jumped up and started filling the little paddling pool. Herbie and Muffin ran straight over to me. I held the hose up, letting them drink from the stream.

Suddenly it felt like a sunshiny, baby-blue-sky day. I let out a happy howl, like a wolf calling to the sunshine-yellow moon.

"Do you know what, Herb and Muff?" I said. "I really hope my dad's having as much fun in Canada! Hop in, little fellows. The water's sublime!"

# Is a Yorkshire terrier the dog for you?

Hi! It's me, Alfreeda!

I'm sure you'd love your own teeny, tiny Yorkie now too, wouldn't you? Of course you would! But actually, Yorkies don't make good pets for all families. So before you run out to buy or adopt one, here are some important facts you should know:

**Yorkies are toy-size dogs and have tiny bones,** ones that can break easily. Tripping over a Yorkie, or sitting on him by accident, can spell B-I-G trouble for such a little dog. If you have young children in your family, get a bigger dog that can handle more of the wild child action.

**Yorkies can be hard to house train.** (That means getting them to go to the loo outside.) Yorkies HATE cold or rainy days. If you live somewhere where it's cold or rains a lot, your Yorkie might not go outside to do her business. (Some families use an indoor litter box or a small doggy door leading to a covered part of the garden.)

**Yorkies HAVE to be brushed or combed every day,** and their hair needs cutting often, too. Their hair is fine and straight, so it gets messy quickly. If you can't promise to brush your dog every day, don't get a Yorkie. Get a hamster.

Okay, signing off for now ... until the next adventure at Hound Hotel!

Yours very factually,

Alfreeda Wolfe

# Glossary

**annoy**  make someone lose patience or feel angry

**creatures**  living beings, human or animal

**demand**  ask or call for with authority

**disgusting**  very unpleasant and offensive to others

**fetch**  go after and bring something or somebody back

**gallop**  run quickly

**howl**  make a loud, sad noise

**overflow**  flow over the edges of something

**shove**  push hard or roughly

**sparkly**  shiny or glittery

**valley**  area of low land between hills

**wonky**  not straight

# Talk about it

1. Which character do you think you are most like and why?

2. What do you think would be the good things and bad things of living next to a dog-boarding kennel?

3. On page 68, Alfreeda has shared some facts (and opinions) about Yorkshire terriers. Do you think a Yorkshire terrier would be a good dog for your family? Why or why not?

# Write about it

1. Think about a time when you felt homesick. Write a paragraph or two comparing how you felt to the way Herbie seems to feel in the story.

2. Write a letter to the twins' dad about Herbie. Use either Alfie's or Alfreeda's point of view.

3. Write a factsheet about Yorkshire terriers. Use three or more reputable sources for your work.

# About the author

Shelley Swanson Sateren grew up with five pet dogs –
a beagle, a terrier mix, a terrier-poodle mix, a
Weimaraner and a German shorthaired pointer. As an
adult, she adopted a lively West Highland white terrier
called Max. Apart from writing many children's books,
Shelley has worked as a children's book editor and in a
children's bookshop. She lives in Minnesota, USA, with
her husband, and has two grown-up sons.

# About the illustrator

Deborah Melmon has worked as an illustrator for over
25 years. After graduating from the Academy of Art
University in San Francisco, she started her career
illustrating covers for a weekly magazine supplement.
Since then, she has produced artwork for over twenty
children's books. Her artwork can also be found on
wrapping paper, greeting cards and fabric. Deborah
lives in California, USA, and shares her studio with an
energetic Airedale terrier called Mack.

ADVENTURES AT HOUND HOTEL
Fearless Freddie
WRITTEN BY Shelley Swanson Sateren
ILLUSTRATION BY Deborah Melmon

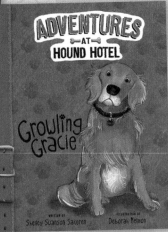

ADVENTURES AT HOUND HOTEL
Growling Gracie
WRITTEN BY Shelley Swanson Sateren
ILLUSTRATION BY Deborah Melmon

ADVENTURES AT HOUND HOTEL
Homesick Herbie
WRITTEN BY Shelley Swanson Sateren
ILLUSTRATION BY Deborah Melmon

ADVENTURES AT HOUND HOTEL
Mudball Molly
WRITTEN BY Shelley Swanson Sateren
ILLUSTRATION BY Deborah Melmon